There's a party in the attic tonight.
And the grown-ups say to the little ones,
"Please behave like ladies and gentlemice."

The grown-ups say to each other,
"How enchanting to see you."
"What's up there? What's up there?"
say the little ones. "LET'S GO UP!"

The grown-ups say to each other,
"Don't you adore a waltz?"
"Boop-a-doop! Boop-a-doop!" say the little
ones. "WHAT'S THROUGH THAT DOOR?"

The grown-ups say to each other,
"Hard work, these parties."
"What fun! What fun!" say the little ones.
"WHAT OTHER FUN CAN WE FIND?"

The grown-ups say to each other, "This room is the heart of the party."
"Where are we? Where are we?" say the little ones. "LET'S EXPLORE SOME MORE!"

"We're explorers! We're explorers!" say
the little ones.
"We even found new friends.
WHAT ELSE CAN WE DISCOVER?"